I Don't Want to Go to School

Helping Children Cope with Separation Anxiety

By
Nancy Pando, LICSW

Illustrations by
Kathy Voerg

New Horizon Press
Far Hills, New Jersey

To Greg, Dickie, Jacqui and Michael
for being my heart and my funny bone.
To Mom and Dad for their once upon a times.
To my family, friends and the children
who helped Honey to be, my love and gratitude.

New Horizon Press
P.O. Box 669
Far Hills, NJ 07931

Pando, Nancy
    I Don't Want to Go to School: Helping Children Cope with Separation Anxiety

Cover Design: Norma Ehrler Rahn
Interior Design: Catherine Finnegan

Library of Congress Control Number: 2004118085

ISBN: 978-0-88282-254-9
SMALL HORIZONS ˉ
A Division of New Horizon Press

14   13   12   /   4   5   6

Honey Maloo, a little bee, lived with her mom in the knothole of a big oak tree. She loved to sing and tap dance. Most of all, she loved staying home with her mother every day and every night. Honey was a very happy bee.

One September day her mother said, "Honey, tomorrow will be your first day of school."

"I don't want to go to school!" shouted Honey. She ran to her room.

Mom came in and sat on the bed. "Honey, do you remember when we met your teacher, Miss Daisy Petal? She seemed very nice."

"Yes, but I don't want to go to school." Honey hid her face in her pillow.

"School will be fun, Honey. Your friends, Binky Bug and Tooty Beetle, will be in your class, too."

The next morning Honey's mom helped the little bee pick out a pink dress and hair bows for her first day of school. Honey went downstairs for breakfast and slowly began eating a bowl of her favorite cereal, Flea Pops, and drinking a tiny glass of orange juice.

"Honey," her mother called. "You must finish your breakfast. We have to be at the bus stop at eight o'clock."

"I don't want to go to school!" Honey said, stamping her tiny foot.

"Honey, you will love school," Mom said.

"I love you better," answered Honey.

Mom stopped and gave Honey a big hug.

"I love you so-o-o much, too, little bee." Patting Honey's head, Mom said, "We both have things we must do today—you have to go to school and I have work to do. If you feel sad, look at your watch. When the big hand points to the twelve and the little hand points to the three, it will be time for you to come home. I will sit and hold you just like I am now."

At the bus stop, Honey and her mother waited. The yellow bus came down the street and stopped. The black rubber doors snapped open. The bus driver got out to help Honey climb in. Mom waved good-bye to Honey and blew a kiss.

The bus whooshed away.

Honey flew right out the bus window and back to her house.

The kitchen window was open. She hopped from the kitchen counter onto the window shade and rolled herself up in it.

Honey whispered to herself, "Yikes! It is dark in here, but it is a good hiding place. No one will be able to see me." She waited and waited. Suddenly, Honey felt like she was going to sneeze.

Ah-h-choo! Honey rolled out of the window shade and fell into the kitchen sink.

Honey's mom was wiping the kitchen counter and saw the little bee. "Honey!" cried Mom. "What are you doing here?" Mom scooped Honey into her arms and hugged her little bee. "I know you want to be with me, but you must go to school, Honey."

"I just want to stay home," sobbed Honey as she wrapped her feelers around her mother's neck.

"Honey," said Mom, wiping away her daughter's tears, "you are not a baby bee anymore. You are a big girl bee and big girl bees go to school."

"Okay," agreed Honey, nodding her head. A tear rolled down her face.

"I am tucking your favorite stuffed flower in your backpack," said Mom. "That way, you can hug and squeeze the flower when you miss me."

Honey nodded her head yes.

"I have to drive you to school now, Honey." Honey made a face, but she went to school with her mom.

On the second day of school, Honey tried again to fly out the school bus window. The bus driver had to stop the bus and tell her to sit down. Miss Petal, Honey's teacher, called Honey's mom to tell her what happened.

When Honey came home from school that afternoon, Mom said, "Honey, you must not fly out the bus window. You can get badly hurt. You have to obey the safety rules."

Mom pulled a yellow handkerchief from her pocket and sprayed it with her honeysuckle perfume. She tucked the handkerchief into Honey's backpack next to the stuffed flower.

The next day at school, Honey sat in the classroom with her arms folded and her head on the desk.

"Honey," asked Miss Petal, "what is the matter?"

"I miss my mom."

"I know, Honey, but now it is time to draw. Would you please get the big box of crayons from my desk?"

"I want to go home right now," said Honey, sticking out her lower lip.

"Unless you are sick," said Miss Petal, "you must stay in school all day."

Early the next morning Honey found her favorite pink marker and drew dots all over her body—even on her pajamas.

"Oh, my," said Mom when she saw Honey. "You have a terrible rash."

"Yes, Mom," said Honey. "My head feels very hot, too. I am sure I will have to stay home today."

"Well," said Mom, pressing her hand against Honey's forehead, "certainly your pajamas will have to stay home, because they have a rash, too."

"Oh, yes," Honey said. Her face got red.

"Honey, you are going to school today with or without your pink marker dots!"

The little bee was very sad. Honey trudged into the classroom and plopped down in her seat. She closed her eyes and covered her ears.

Just then, Mr. Pottinger, the dragonfly who taught the class music, was rolling his keyboard into the room. He looked at the little bee.

"What is wrong with Honey?" he asked.

Honey's teacher, Miss Petal, sighed. "I am afraid Honey misses her mother," said Miss Petal. "She does not want to be here."

Mr. Pottinger turned to the class. "Well," he said, "does anyone have any ideas about how to help Honey feel better?"

"I do," answered Tooty Beetle. "I hum my favorite song when I start missing my family."

"I talk to my friends," said Binky Bug.

"I play ball at recess," said Mooky Caterpillar.

"Honey," said Mr. Pottinger, "those are all very good ideas. What could you do to help yourself feel better?"

Suddenly, Honey remembered the things her mother had put in her backpack. "I could squeeze my favorite stuffed flower! Maybe I could smell my mother's handkerchief!" She thought very hard. "Oh, I can check my watch so I will know what time I will see my mom again." She was very proud of herself for remembering these things.

"You are a very brave and strong little bee," said Mr. Pottinger. "Since you are strong on the inside, you must have a strong voice on the outside. Do you like to sing?" he asked her.

"Yes, I love to sing!" Honey replied.

"Then I will give you a special song about a rose to sing in our school concert." Mr. Pottinger went on, "Everybody will perform in our concert. We need to practice, so let us get started."

In the play, Mooky caterpillar was supposed to be a rock and sit still. Instead he kept jumping up and down. Binky Bug was supposed to hold up the sun so it would shine during the song. She dropped it on Tooty's head three times. Tooty Beetle was supposed to squirt water on the flowers. He accidentally squirted Mr. Pottinger. Even Honey had trouble remembering the words to her rose song.

"Do not worry, class," said Mr. Pottinger. "If we keep practicing, you will all do a very good job at our concert."

For the next few weeks Miss Petal helped the class learn their letters and numbers. Every day the class practiced their singing.

One night Honey told her mother about the concert. "I get to be a rose and sing a special song," she announced.

"It sounds like you enjoy music class," Mom said.

"I do, but I still miss you," Honey answered.

On the morning of the concert, Honey came downstairs and said, "I don't feel like going to school today. My tummy feels funny."

"Why does your tummy feel funny?" asked Mom.

"I think it might be afraid to sing in the concert," said Honey.

"Maybe your tummy will feel better if you eat a bowl of Flea Pops," Mom said, pouring cereal for Honey. "Everyone feels nervous when they are in a play, Honey Bee," explained Mom. "I have a present that might make you feel better."

"What?" Honey asked excitedly.

Honey's eyes widened as her mother handed her a small wrapped box. Inside the box was a pretty gold locket shaped like a heart.

Honey opened the locket. Inside was a picture of Honey on one side and her mom on the other side. When Honey closed the locket, the two pictures were hugging each other.

At school that afternoon, Miss Petal helped all the little bugs and bees put on their costumes. Honey was dressed as a yellow rose. She fluffed her petals and smoothed her leaves.

Honey wore the locket around her neck and showed it to all her school friends. Miss Petal liked the locket, too.

"Do you feel better about school now?" asked Miss Petal.

"Yes," said Honey. "I have my favorite stuffed flower, my mom's perfumed handkerchief and my watch that tells me when I am going home."

"Wonderful," said Miss Petal.

"Okay, everybody!" Miss Petal called. "It's showtime!"

On stage, Mr. Pottinger placed his sheet music on the keyboard. The curtain opened. The concert began.

Everybody in the class remembered the words to the songs. Mooky Caterpillar, the rock, stayed very still. Binky Bug held up the shining sun and held it high during the whole concert. Tooty Beetle, the rain cloud, squirted water on the flowers. Mr. Pottinger smiled, because he stayed dry.

Then Honey stepped up to the microphone to sing her special song. Her voice was loud and strong. Everyone clapped when the song was over.

Honey heard Mom call out, "Bravo, Honey Bee!" And Honey bowed.

When the concert ended and the curtain closed, the little bees and bugs hurried into the auditorium to greet their parents. Everyone told them the concert was wonderful.

Honey kissed and hugged her mother. "Mom, I love school," she said and buzzed back to class. She could hear Mom down the hall singing, "Three cheers for Honey Bee Maloo and every one of you!"

THE END

TIPS FOR KIDS

1. It is okay to feel sad. When you do, talk about your feelings to a special adult or friend who will try to help you.

2. Get busy doing something; it makes the time go by more quickly.

3. You are very brave and can get through this. Take some deep breaths and remember, there have been other times in your life when you have shown your bravery. Do it again.

4. Think of a story you can tell your parents when you see them again.

5. Hug yourself.

6. Go play with kids who make you feel happy.

7. Bring something from home to keep with you. Some of the things you can bring: a teddy bear, a picture of you hugging your parents, a piece of your favorite blanket to keep in your pocket, Mom's scarf with her perfume on it (when you breathe her smell, it goes straight down to your heart).

8. Look up at the sky—then catch the kiss Mom or Dad is sending you right now.

9. Look at the clock and find the number when you will see your mom or dad again.

10. Remember, sad feelings do not stay for long.

TIPS FOR PARENTS

1. You are likely doing something very right for your child to feel so attached. Remember, some children simply adjust to change better than others. After you leave, your child's sadness will often dissipate.

2. Look at the period of time when the child is coping during the day, then ask the child, "How did you get to be so strong as to get through sad times?" The object is to get the child to name his or her strengths—then build on them.

3. Children are very concrete. Give your child visual reminders of when you will be together again: watches, clocks with a sticker on the hour of your return, calendars with drawings. Show your child where you are when you are not with him or her (e.g., your workplace).

4. Transitional objects can be very helpful: stuffed animals, a scarf sprayed with your perfume (our sense of smell is most powerfully connected to memories), a picture of you and your child hugging, a piece of your inexpensive jewelry that will fit into a pocket, a piece of his or her security blanket. For older children who prefer discretion, pin something to the inside of their shirts; it is close to the heart.

5. Set limits on your good-byes. Prepare the child briefly, then stop talking about the departure. Be loving and confident: three kisses, three hugs... then go! Lingering around good-byes only increases a child's anxiety.

6. Tell your child when you will be back—"When the teacher says it is time to go... after lunch...when the bus comes...when the sun disappears," et cetera.

7. Start a project that involves you and your child. Tell him or her that you would like to work on it when you are together again.

8. Familiarize your child with any new setting prior to the actual start day. If possible, make the introductions to other children for your child.

9. Tell your child to look up at the sky when he or she misses you and at that exact time you will be sending a kiss.

10. It is perfectly normal for children to experience separation anxiety. If this phase continues in its acute stage for more than one month, consult with a mental health professional who specializes in children to determine if clinical intervention is needed.